Dear Parents and Educators,

W9-BSW-601

Welcome to Penguin Young Readers! As parents and educators, you know that each child develops at his or her own pace—in terms of speech, critical thinking, and, of course, reading. Penguin Young Readers recognizes this fact. As a result, each Penguin Young Readers book is assigned a traditional easy-to-read level (1–4) as well as a Guided Reading Level (A–P). Both of these systems will help you choose the right book for your child. Please refer to the back of each book for specific leveling information. Penguin Young Readers features esteemed authors and illustrators, stories about favorite characters, fascinating nonfiction, and more!

Max & Ruby™: Fireman Max

LEVEL 2

GUIDED READING LEVEL **I**

This book is perfect for a **Progressing Reader** who:
• can figure out unknown words by using picture and context clues;
• can recognize beginning, middle, and ending sounds;
• can make and confirm predictions about what will happen in the text; and
• can distinguish between fiction and nonfiction.

Here are some **activities** you can do during and after reading this book:
• Compound Words: A compound word is made when two words are joined together to form a new word. Reread the story to find the compound words. On a separate piece of paper, write down each word that makes up the compound word. Find the definition for each word and use each word in a sentence.
• Compare/Contrast: Max and Ruby are brother and sister. Sometimes they get along, and other times they don't. Make a list of ways in which they are alike, and ways in which they are different.

Remember, sharing the love of reading with a child is the best gift you can give!

—Bonnie Bader, EdM
  Penguin Young Readers program

*Penguin Young Readers are leveled by independent reviewers applying the standards developed by Irene Fountas and Gay Su Pinnell in *Matching Books to Readers: Using Leveled Books in Guided Reading*, Heinemann, 1999.

PENGUIN YOUNG READERS
Published by the Penguin Group
Penguin Group (USA) LLC, 375 Hudson Street, New York, New York 10014, USA

USA | Canada | UK | Ireland | Australia | New Zealand | India | South Africa | China

penguin.com
A Penguin Random House Company

ISBN 978-0-448-48927-8   10 9 8 7 6 5 4 3 2 1

Fireman Max

Penguin Young Readers
An Imprint of Penguin Group (USA) LLC

Max is playing fireman.

He has a red fireman's hat

and a fire truck.

"Fireman!" says Max.

The fire truck rolls away.

Ruby jumps rope with Louise.

Louise jumps while Ruby swings
the rope.

"One, two, three," Ruby counts.

Louise misses a jump.

"Now it's your turn, Ruby!"

"Fireman!" shouts Max.

Ruby misses her jump.

"Max," says Ruby, "can you

play fireman somewhere else?"

Max plays with his fire truck.

"Vroom, vroom! Fireman!"

says Max.

Max pushes the fire truck

toward Ruby.

She misses another jump.

"Max," says Ruby, "can you
play with your fire truck
somewhere else?"

Max goes to the sandbox.

He plays with the fire truck's

white hose.

It is short.

Max finds a green hose.

It is long.

Ruby starts to jump again.

"One . . ."

Max bumps into Ruby

with the long green hose.

"Max," says Ruby, "can you

play somewhere else?"

Max plays with the yellow

ladder on his fire truck.

It is small.

Max finds another ladder.

It is tall.

"Fireman!" says Max.

Ruby starts to jump again.

"One . . ."

Max bumps into Louise
with the ladder.

"Max," says Ruby, "can you
play somewhere else?"

"Look, Max.

You have lots of toys to play

with over here," says Ruby.

"You can pretend there is a fire
in the sandbox, and use your
trucks to put it out," says Ruby.

Max plays with his toys in the sandbox.

They all drive away!

Bunny Scout Leader comes

to watch Ruby and Louise

jump rope.

Ruby starts to jump.

The fire truck goes

toward Ruby.

Ruby jumps over it.

"One!" Louise says.

The white ambulance goes

toward Ruby.

Ruby jumps again.

"Two!" says Louise.

The black-and-white

police car goes toward Ruby.

Ruby jumps again.

"Three!" says Louise.

The trucks come back.

Ruby has to jump again.

"Come on, Ruby!"

Bunny Scout Leader says.

"You can do it!"

"Four, five, six!"

says Louise.

The trucks come back

one more time.

"Seven, eight, nine," says Ruby.

"I did it!"

"What a fun jumping game,"

says Bunny Scout Leader.

"What do you call it?"

"Fireman!" says Max.